D1351085

BEARS ON WHEELS

by Stan and Jan Berenstain

COLLINS

1 2 3 4 5 6 7 8 9 10

ISBN 0 00 171289 6 (paperback)

ISBN 0 00 171206 3 (hardback)

A Bright and Early Book for Beginning Beginners
Published by arrangement with Random House Inc.,
New York, New York
First Published in Great Britain 1970
Printed in Great Britain by
William Collins Sons & Co Ltd, Glasgow

One bear.

One wheel.

One bear on one wheel.

Two bears on one wheel.

Three on one.

Four on one.

Four bears on one wheel.

One bear on two wheels.

Four on two.

One on one again.

One on one.

Three on three.

None on four.

Four on none.

One on one again.

Five on one.

Five bears on one.

Five bears on none.

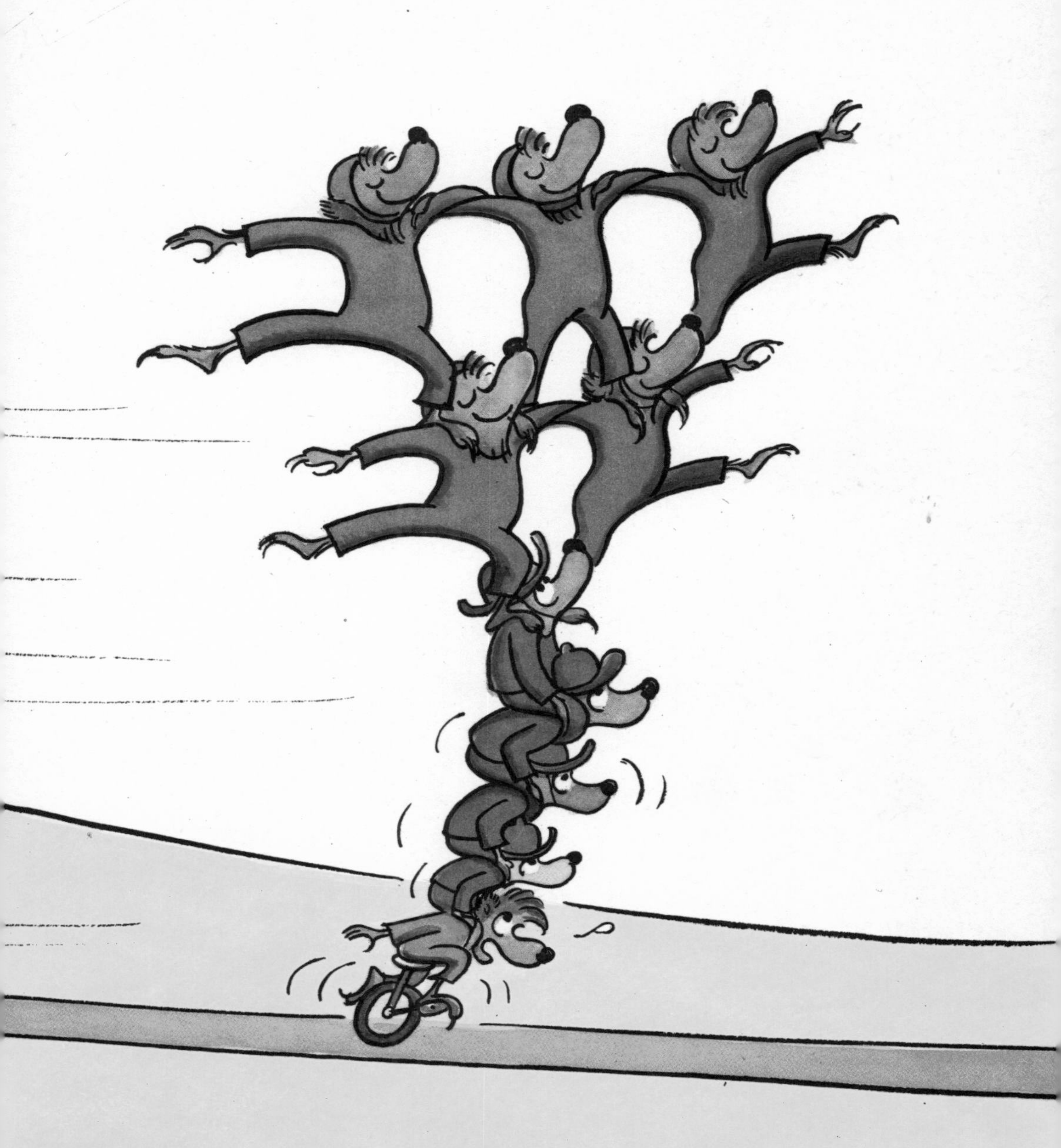

Ten on one.

One bear on five wheels.

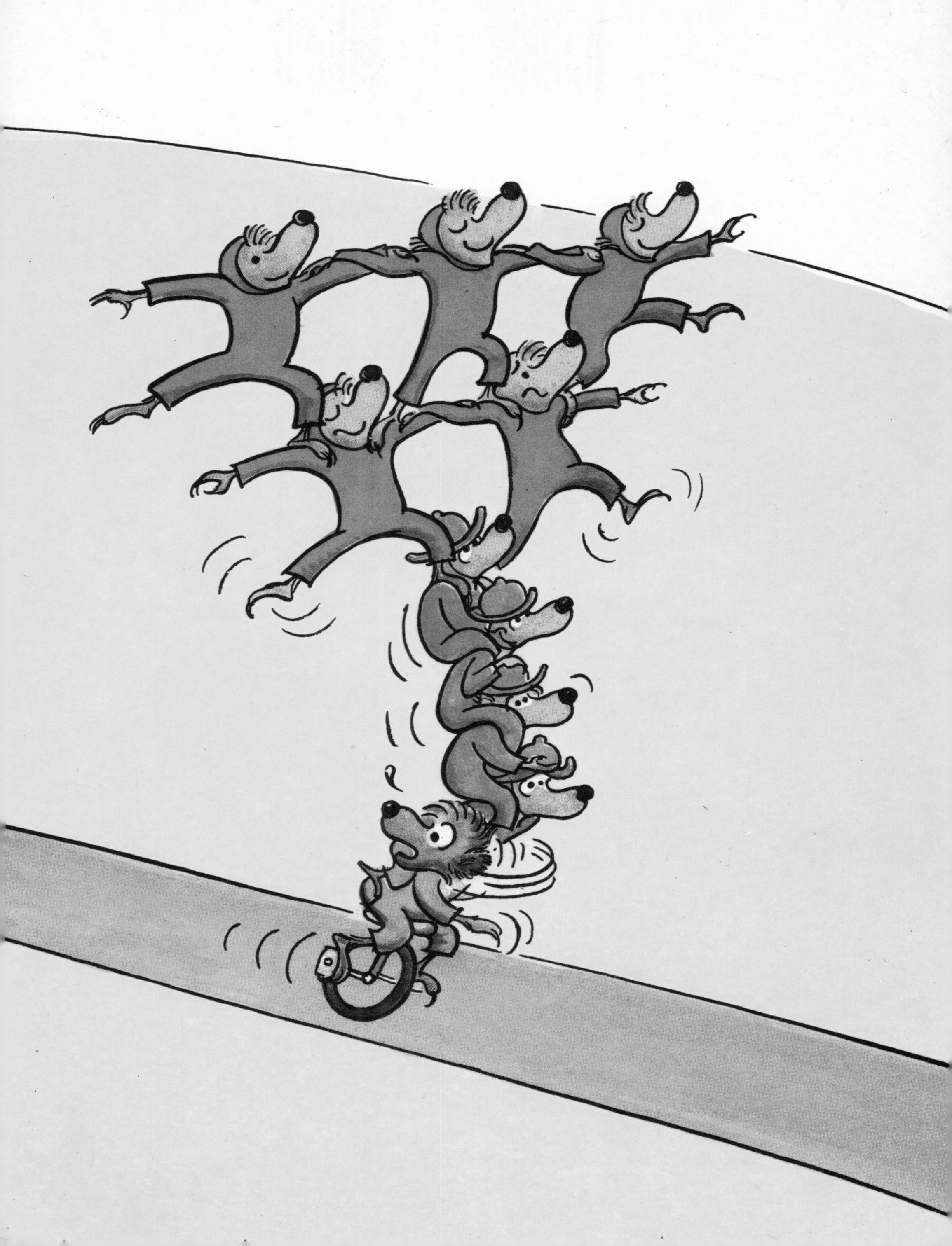

One on five.

Ten on one.

Ten on ten.

Twenty-one on none.

One on one again.